Contents

Shep
Focus on: sh as in *shop* 3

Check on the chicks!
Focus on: ch as in *chip* 8

Shep and me
Focus on: th as in *that* 13

Lots of legs
Focus on: th as in *thing* 18

Scan to listen along!
Audio to accompany this book can be streamed online with a mobile or tablet using this QR code:

About this book

These short stories are designed to give young children blending and reading practice. They are decodable, which means the words in them only include letter shapes and sounds that the children have learned. The stories also gradually introduce a few 'tricky' words, which are essential for children to become familiar with, such as 'they', 'of' and 'said'.

As children progress through these readers, new letter sounds and 'tricky' words are added and previous learning is revised. The progression links directly to the teaching order and lessons in the Letterland *Teacher's Guides* (UK and US versions). Each story begins with a title page that provides important information for children and teachers.

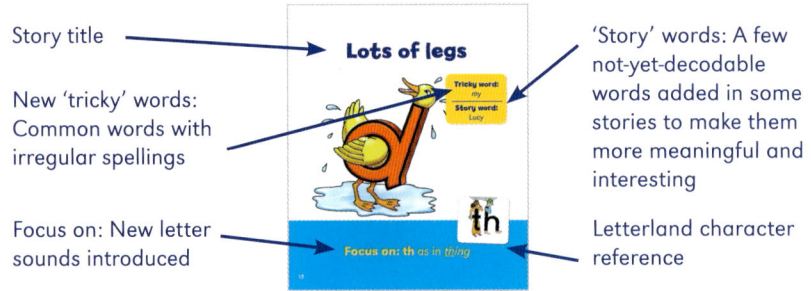

Basic teaching tips:

- Encourage the sounding out of decodable words (and any decodable parts of 'tricky' words).
- Discuss the stories with the children to ensure comprehension and engagement.
- Encourage re-reading in pairs or individually to develop fluency and reading for meaning.

See **www.letterland.com/Phonics-Readers** and the latest editions of the Letterland **Teacher's Guides** for more suggestions on how to use this book.

Shep

Focus on: sh as in *shop*

I got Shep at the pet shop.

We go to the dock.
We like to see the ships.

Shep has a big dish.

Shep likes to nap.
Hush!

Check on the chicks!

Focus on: ch as in *chip*

He is checking on the pen.
He sees chicks on the run.

He picks up the chicks.

He chops the logs.
He has a lot to chop.

He packs the... shhh!

Shep and me

Tricky word: my

Focus on: th as in *that*

This is my dog Shep and me.
We have lots of fun.

She naps in that shed.

Then she gets up.
Sit up, Shep. That's it!

I hug Shep.
She licks my chin. Ug!

Lots of legs

Story word: Lucy

Focus on: th as in *thing*

Ed has a bath.
Ed has thick legs.

The duck likes to get wet.
She has thin legs.

Lucy is on the path.
She has long legs!

Lucy sees this thing on the path. It has 100 legs.

About this series

This series consists of 20 books which are divided into four sets. Each book contains a selection of short stories, featuring the phonic elements listed below. In total there are 83 engaging stories that children can use to decode the 44 sounds of the English language. For more information, see **www.letterland.com/Phonics-Readers**

Set	Book	No. of stories	Focus elements	As in the word...
1	a	4	c, a, d, h, m, t, s, i, s	cat, add, dog, hen, map, tap, sun, it, is
	b	4	i, i, n, g	it, ice, net, go
	c	4	o, o, p, s, s	odd, so, pen, cats, dogs
	d	4	e, e, ss, u	egg, he, miss, up
	e	4	u, k, ck, ng	uniform, kit, duck, ring
2	a	4	sh, ch, th, th	shop, chip, that, thing
	b	4	l, f, ff, ll, b	leg, fan, puff, bell, bat
	c	4	j, all, r, qu	jet, ball, run, quiz
	d	4	v, ve, o, w	van, have, son, wig
	e	4	x, y, z	box, yes, zip
3	a	5	sl, sp, st, sw, sk, sm, sn, cl, fl, pl, bl, gl, br, cr, dr, fr, gr, tr	slip, spot, stuck, swim, skate, smash, snap, clock, flag, plug, block, glad, brick, crab, drip, frog, grin, track
	b	4	cr, dr, fr, gr, nd, nk, nt, y	crab, drip, frog, grin, hand, tank, tent, my
	c	5	a_e, i_e, e_e, o_e, u_e, ed, ed, ed	make, like, these, home, cube, skated, smiled, hoped
	d	4	ed, ed, ed, y, ai, ay, ee	landed, clapped, slammed, baby, rain, say, bee
	e	4	ea, oa, ie, ue	sea, boat, tie, blue
4	a	4	ild, ind, old, ar, or	mild, kind, cold, farm, for
	b	3	ir, ur, er	girl, fur, her
	c	4	ow, igh	show, night
	d	4	oo, oo, u, aw, au, ew, ew	moon, book, put, saw, cause, few, grew
	e	6	ow, ou, oy, oi, air, ear	how, out, boy, coin, fair, year

Titles in this series

Set 1
· Sam and other stories
· Nat and other stories
· Go, pup, go! and other stories
· Pets and other stories
· Can he kick? and other stories

Set 2
· Shep and me and other stories
· Is this her pet? and other stories
· Red Robot runs and other stories
· Hugs and other stories
· Zig and Zag and other stories

Set 3
· Spin and smash and other stories
· Can a crab grab? and other stories
· Rose bakes a cake and other stories
· Look what happened! and other stories
· Molly and me by the sea and other stories

Set 4
· Carly and the sharks and other stories
· My very bad morning and other stories
· Ben's birthday surprise and other stories
· Penguins on the loose and other stories
· What big flippers you have and other stories

Published by Letterland International Ltd. 8/10 South Street, Epsom, Surrey, KT18 7PF, UK
© Letterland International 2013. Reprinted 2017, 2018, 2019, 2020, 2021.
10 9 8 7

Sold as part of Set 2. ISBN: 978-1-86209-892-3, Product Code: TE11
This book ISBN: 978-1-86209-900-5, Product Code: TE19
LETTERLAND™ is a trademark of Letterland International Ltd.
Printed in China

Author: Stamey Carter
Editor: Lyn Wendon
Originator of Letterland: Lyn Wendon
Artwork: Baz Rowell
Design: Beth Maddox

The author asserts the moral right to be identified as the author of this work.
All rights reserved. No part of this publication may be reproduced, stored in a retrieval system, or transmitted in any form or by any means, electronic, mechanical, photocopying, recording or otherwise, without either the prior permission of the Publisher or a licence permitting restricted copying in the United Kingdom issued by the Copyright Licensing Agency Ltd, 90 Tottenham Court Road, London W1T 4LP. This book is sold subject to the condition that it shall not by way of trade or otherwise be lent, hired out or otherwise circulated without the Publisher's prior consent.